SADDLEBACK STABLES

Biscuit Shrinks

Written by Lisa Thompson

Illustrated by Molly Sage

Blake
EDUCATION
Better ways to learn

Saddleback Stables: Biscuit Shrinks
ISBN: 978 1 76020 169 2

Lexile®Measure: 710L
For more information visit www.lexile.com
Lexile © 2013 MetaMetrics, Inc.

Text copyright © 2018 Lisa Thompson
Written by Lisa Thompson
Illustrations copyright © 2018 Blake Publishing
Illustrated by Molly Sage

Published by Blake Education Pty Ltd
ABN 50 074 266 023
108 Main Road
Clayton South VIC 3169
info@blake.com.au
www.blake.com.au

Publisher: Katy Pike
Series editor: Mark Stafford
Page layout: Modern Art Production Group
Printer: 1010 Printing Asia Limited

CONTENTS

Jordy

Chief

Sophie

Biscu

Hannah

Jin Jin

Bella

Gypsy Rose

Alexa

Billy Blaze

4

CHAPTER ONE

Farewell

Jimmy, the farrier, had been busy all morning at Saddleback Stables. He was shoeing ponies and horses and trimming their hooves. Jimmy had just finished shoeing Billy Blaze, which was Alexa MacKenzie's horse. Billy Blaze behaved **perfectly**, so Jimmy gave him a mint as a reward.

"You know," said Alexa, "I really don't think you should give treats unless they're **earned** during training. A horse shouldn't be spoiled."

Hannah and Bella watched from the other end of the stables. They glanced at each other. Alexa had lots of rules about caring for ponies and horses.

"But I guess Billy Blaze kept still while he got his new shoes," said Alexa.

"That he did," said Jimmy. He rubbed Billy Blaze's neck, untied him and handed Alexa the lead rope. Alexa led him out to his paddock.

Jimmy looked over at Bill, the manager of Saddleback Stables. "Right-o, Bill, who's up next? What about that skewbald pony, **Jim Jim**?"

Hannah giggled. "You mean **Jin Jin**. I'll go get him."

Jin Jin belonged to Saddleback Stables but ever since Hannah began riding him, she felt like he was **hers**. They had a **special bond**. Hannah lived just up the road and visited Jin Jin most days after school. She also had a riding lesson every Saturday with her stable friends Bella, Sophie and Jordy. Alexa had private lessons.

Miss Jill, the chief riding instructor and owner of Saddleback Stables, asked Hannah to visit especially this afternoon. She wanted Hannah to keep Jin Jin calm while Jimmy worked on him. Jin Jin didn't wear shoes but he needed his hooves trimmed.

Out in the paddock, Hannah clipped a lead rope to her pony's halter. "Come on, Jin Jin. It's **pony pedicure time**."

Jin Jin wouldn't move. He knew something was up. Hannah looked over her shoulder to make sure Alexa wasn't around, and slipped Jin Jin two pieces of dried apple. That got him moving but his ears were **twitching**.

"Jin Jin, you're going to be fine," said Hannah as she led him to the stables. "Your hooves just need a little trim … but I could ask Jimmy to paint them. Would you like that?"

Hannah tied Jin Jin to the rail for Jimmy. The farrier ran his kind hands down Jin Jin's shoulder, then lifted a leg and got to work.

"The edge of a hoof is just like one of our fingernails or toenails," Jimmy said as he cut, filed and shaped. "If we don't look after them, they'll crack and cause problems. If a hoof gets too long and splits, it **hurts**."

Jin Jin was tense. Hannah stroked his neck and she felt him relax.

Jimmy worked his way around Jin Jin, hoof by hoof. "Always keep an eye on the condition of your pony's hooves. You don't want him coming up lame." He put the last hoof down. "I'm glad to say this pony's hooves are now in **tiptop condition**. We're friends for life now, aren't we Jin Jin."

Jimmy slipped Jin Jin a mint, just like he had given Billy Blaze.

"I think you might be," said Hannah, watching the mint disappear behind Jin Jin's lips.

Hannah saw Sophie as she led Jin Jin back to his paddock. Sophie was the first friend Hannah made at Saddleback Stables. Jin Jin shared a paddock with Biscuit, the pony Sophie rode. Biscuit was a **scruffy** chestnut-coloured Shetland pony. Like Jin Jin, Biscuit belonged to the stables; like Hannah, Sophie felt like he was her very own.

As Hannah got closer she saw Sophie was crying as she brushed Biscuit.

"Sophie, what's wrong? Why are you crying?"

"I've come to say goodbye," **sniffed** Sophie.

"What? What do you mean?"

"My dad got a new job and we have to move. We leave on Monday. I came to say goodbye to everyone … **especially** Biscuit. I don't know what I'm going to do without him." Sophie wiped at her tears as she stroked Biscuit's soft nose.

Hannah didn't know what to say. She hugged her friend. Sophie had ridden Biscuit every week for over a year. Hannah had known Jin Jin for only a month but she knew she'd be **heartbroken** if she left Saddleback Stables!

Everyone gathered to say goodbye to Sophie. They hugged, wished her well, and promised they would take extra care of Biscuit.

The next day, Biscuit was quiet because Sophie didn't come to see him. Another day passed and then a whole week. Biscuit ate less and less. He stood by himself in a corner of the paddock, his head down.

Bill assured everyone Biscuit would be his old self in another week. Hannah and Bella took him for rides, and Jordy stopped for a chat and to pat him whenever he passed. Jin Jin teased him by **nipping** at his tail. Bill hung around Biscuit's paddock at feed time, to make sure he ate.

But by the end of the week, Biscuit was not his usual, cheeky self. He was eating a little more but he was slow to move and looked **miserable**.

Alexa had an idea to help Biscuit get his **spark** back, so she went to see Bill and Miss Jill.

CHAPTER TWO

Poor Biscuit

"The nerve of her!" huffed Bella when she heard about Alexa's plan.

Bella, Jordy and Hannah walked their ponies slowly towards the stables.

"Sophie has only been gone two weeks and Alexa has already organised for someone to **replace her**!" continued Bella. "She insists Biscuit needs a new 'special rider' as soon as possible. Well, she never called Sophie a 'special rider'. She called her a 'borrower'. Alexa gave Sophie such a **hard time** about riding a stable pony."

"Alexa calls anyone who doesn't own

a pony or horse a borrower," Jordy said and shrugged. "I'm a borrower and it doesn't bug me."

"It bugged Sophie," growled Bella, "and whoever this new person is won't even be in our Saturday class. Apparently she'll have private lessons, like Alexa. I can't imagine what Sophie would think if she knew!"

Jordy leaned forward and rubbed Chief's neck. "Biscuit needs a new rider, Bella, and not just the occasional trail rider. I think it **could** be a good thing."

Bella huffed. "What do you think, Hannah?"

Hannah understood Bella wanted her to be as annoyed with Alexa as she was, especially in front of Jordy. She was surprised that Alexa had found a new rider for Biscuit, and agreed that Alexa was rude to call people borrowers. It made sense that Bella was upset. But Jordy had a point: maybe a new rider was just what Biscuit needed.

Hannah didn't get a chance to explain her thoughts. Just as she was about to answer, a large, red four-wheel drive **rumbled** past the ponies in a cloud of dust. It pulled up next to Biscuit's paddock and three people climbed out: Alexa's mum, Alexa in her shiny riding boots and perfect ponytail, and a small girl with long brown plaits. The newcomer wore jeans, old riding boots and a hoodie. Alexa called Biscuit over to the fence. Hannah

noticed that Alexa's mum had to **coax** the girl to pat the pony. She looked unsure about what she was doing.

Alexa walked off towards the tack room. "Come on, guys," said Bella. "Let's find out about this *special* rider. I'm sure Alexa's **dying** to tell us."

"Lola is a very good friend of mine," explained Alexa, as she sorted through riding hats in the tack room. "She's shy, which makes it hard for her to make friends. Having Biscuit as a friend will be good for her. I mean, look at Billy Blaze and me. He's my **best friend**."

Alexa became frustrated as she tossed aside helmets. "I don't know why Lola insists on borrowing a helmet. I offered her one of my old ones to keep." She picked up a **battered** blue helmet, looked at it and pulled a face. "This one will have to do."

Bella was about to say something but Hannah spoke first.

"Has Lola ever ridden before?" she asked.

"A bit," answered Alexa. She collected a saddle, rug and bridle hanging on the wall. "Anyway, I can't stand around here all day. Oh, Bella, I noticed you didn't get shoes put on Gypsy Rose. I don't think I would have done that."

"Gypsy Rose doesn't need shoes," said Bella quickly. "Ponies only need shoes if they walk on roads or rocky trails."

"Well, keep an eye on her hooves then," said Alexa casually. "Billy Blaze needs shoes, seeing as he's a **Show horse**, not a trail pony. Gypsy Rose could be a good show pony with the right rider." She walked **briskly** out of the tack room towards Biscuit's paddock.

"Oh, she is so annoying!" said Bella.

Jordy smiled and plunged his hands into his pockets. "What does she mean 'the right rider'?" Bella continued. "She thinks she knows **everything** about ponies and horses. Well, Gypsy Rose doesn't need shoes and Biscuit doesn't need a new special rider friend!"

Bella snatched up a saddle and bridle and stormed out of the tack room, heading for Gypsy Rose's paddock.

Hannah and Jordy hung back near the stables and watched Alexa adjust Biscuit's saddle for Lola. Lola patted Biscuit's scruffy neck. She climbed into the saddle. She squeezed her heels and Biscuit began to walk around the paddock.

Hannah thought Lola looked comfortable on the Shetland pony.

What's more, Biscuit was enjoying the **attention**. He broke into a trot, and Lola **effortlessly** rose and fell with his rhythm. Biscuit hadn't moved so well, nor held his head so high, since Sophie left.

With Lola in the saddle, Biscuit had a bit of his spark back.

CHAPTER THREE

A New Rider

Lola became a regular at Saddleback Stables. Every week she visited three times after school and once on Saturday to ride Biscuit. Months went by. Lola kept mostly to herself— sometimes she nodded shyly and smiled to the others, but mostly she focused on Biscuit. Lola even began **jumping** with Biscuit, something Sophie had never done.

"I wonder what Sophie would think about Biscuit becoming a bit of a jumping star," said Hannah one afternoon, as she and Bella brushed their ponies. They watched Lola and

Biscuit canter between jumps in the arena.

"I have to admit Lola's a good rider," said Bella, "but Biscuit will always be Sophie's pony to me."

Someone's whistle **rang out** over Saddleback Stables.

"Hey, that sounds like …" Bella stopped herself. "It can't be!"

"Sophie?" said Hannah, looking around. "Sophie whistles like that."

"It is!" cried Bella. "It's Sophie! Look!" Bella waved **frantically** as Sophie ran towards them.

Sophie looked a little different—she was taller and her hair was longer—but she had the same enormous smile. She wrapped her friends in a hug.

"What are you doing here?" asked Bella. "We've missed you *so* much."

"Well, you won't miss me anymore," said Sophie excitedly, "because we're **moving back**! I moaned every day about how much I missed this place and Biscuit. Turns out Mum and Dad weren't happy either. **Parents**! So we packed up and here I am! Everything is going to be just as it was before. Hey, where's Biscuit?"

Bella and Hannah swapped glances as Sophie scanned Saddleback Stables. She spotted Biscuit in the arena.

"Who's riding Biscuit?"

"That's Lola," said Bella.

"Um, Alexa asked her to ride Biscuit after you left," said Hannah.

"Alexa?" Sophie's smile disappeared.

"Biscuit was really missing you," explained Hannah. "Lola is really good with him."

"Really?"

"Lola's **super-shy**," said Bella. "She keeps to herself and Biscuit, mostly."

The disappointment on Sophie's face was obvious.

"Well, look who we have here!" said Miss Jill as she joined the girls. "You're back, Sophie! Your mum called and said you'd be dropping by. How about we get Biscuit over here to see you?"

Miss Jill called out to Lola. As Biscuit walked towards Sophie, he **whinnied** and **bobbed** his head with glee.

"He certainly hasn't forgotten you," said Miss Jill.

Biscuit sniffed Sophie and snorted gently. Sophie rubbed his nose and tickled him between the ears. She pulled a mint from her pocket for him. "I missed you so much, Biscuit," she whispered.

Sophie looked up and smiled at Lola sitting in the saddle. "Hi, I'm Sophie. You're Lola?" Lola nodded and smiled. "Would you mind if I had a little ride of Biscuit?"

Lola dismounted without a word. Bella handed Sophie her helmet and Sophie climbed onto Biscuit. She looked down—her feet hung well below the stirrups. When she put them in the stirrups, her knees bent up at a **funny angle**. She bent down to adjust the stirrup straps and almost fell off.

"Sophie," said Miss Jill, "either Biscuit has shrunk while you were away or you've grown a *lot*. I can adjust those straps a bit but you may now be too big for him."

Sophie slid off Biscuit. She had grown too big to ride her favourite pony.

CHAPTER FOUR

A Best Friend

Sophie rode Reba for the next Saturday morning class. Reba was the stable pony Bella rode before she got Gypsy Rose. She was gentle but old and a **little slow**. Sophie pretended everything was fine, but she didn't have her usual spark.

After the class, Sophie walked Reba slowly back to the stables. Hannah and Bella trotted up on their ponies.

"You can take Gypsy Rose for a ride this afternoon," offered Bella.

"No, I'm alright," sighed Sophie.

"We know you're not," said Hannah.

The girls slid off their ponies outside the stables and tied them up.

"When I was away …" Sophie began. She paused and took a deep breath. "All I could think about was getting back here and riding Biscuit. Now I'm back, things are **different**. I've grown a bit. Lola's riding Biscuit. And I don't have a pony to ride, really. Reba just gets along until class is over." Sophie patted the old grey pony's neck. "Everything has changed."

"Not everything," said Bella. "We haven't changed."

Miss Jill pulled up outside the stables in her four-wheel drive pulling a horse float. Jordy was in the passenger seat.

"Girls," she said, leaning out the window, "please don't go home just yet. I'll need you here this afternoon when I get back, especially you, Sophie. We won't be long."

"I don't know why she needs me," sighed Sophie, as Miss Jill drove off.

Bill **Strode** out of the stables. "Could two of you young ladies give me a hand? I need help in the storeroom."

"I'll put the ponies back," Bella suggested to her friends, "while you help Bill."

Bella walked into the stables and was soon joined by Alexa.

"It must be hard for Sophie," Alexa said, "to come back and see Lola riding Biscuit so well, but I'm sure it was meant to be. **Especially** with Sophie outgrowing Biscuit while she was away. I mean, Lola and Biscuit really do have a **great connection**."

"I'm surprised you think that," said Bella.

"What do you mean?" asked Alexa, a little shocked.

"Well, Lola is a *borrower,* and we know what you think about them— they can't have a special connection because their ponies belong to the stables. You called me a **borrower** before I got Gypsy Rose. You've *always* called Sophie a borrower, like it's a bad thing, like you're better. You're not better because you own Billy Blaze or because Billy Blaze is a horse. You're **not better** than the rest of us, Alexa MacKenzie, and I don't know why you think you are!"

Alexa opened her mouth to say something but shut it again.

"Excuse me," came a whisper. Lola stood at the stable door. She looked worried. "Do you know where Bill is? I need him right away."

"Is everything alright?" asked Alexa.

"Something's wrong with Biscuit," said Lola. "He started **limping** when I put him back in the paddock."

"I'll have a look at him," said Alexa. "Come on, Lola."

"I'll tell Bill to meet you in Biscuit's paddock," said Bella.

Hannah, Sophie and Bella followed Bill to check on Biscuit. The girls stood by the fence as Bill checked Biscuit's hooves one by one. He ran his hand

32

along Biscuit's back as he walked, so he didn't **startle** him. He stayed close to his hind legs in case Biscuit tried to kick him.

"Ah, here's the problem," said Bill finally. "He's got a small crack in his front hoof. I'll give it a bit of a file. He'll be **right as rain**."

Lola sighed with relief and pressed her face against Biscuit's cheek. "Thank goodness you're going to be alright."

Sophie watched as Biscuit's eyelids **drooped** happily.

"He likes you a lot," said Sophie.

"I tell Biscuit everything," said Lola, smiling. "He's my best friend."

Sophie could see how much Biscuit and Lola meant to each other. She was a little sad that Biscuit wasn't only hers any longer, but she was also glad Lola **really** cared for him and Biscuit was happy.

Sophie wrapped Biscuit's neck in a hug as Lola patted him.

35

CHAPTER FIVE

New Beginnings

Everyone was walking back from Biscuit's paddock when Miss Jill's four-wheel drive returned.

"Come on," said Sophie, "let's find out what they've been up to."

They gathered around Miss Jill's horse float and watched quietly as Jordy lowered the float's ramp.

Miss Jill led out a pony with a **golden caramel** coat, **delicate** hooves, and a **creamy white** mane and tail.

Hannah had seen horses like that in books at home—she knew it was a palomino. The pony shone cream and gold in the sunlight and she tossed her silky mane. She held her head proudly, like Alexa's Billy Blaze, but her face was more curved and the tip of her nose was slightly darker. Her nostrils wriggled sensitively in the fresh air.

"Everyone," announced Miss Jill, "I'd like you to meet the newest member of the Saddleback Stables family. This is Peaches. Sophie, you're going to be taking care of her, now that you're not riding Biscuit."

"Really?" cried Sophie.

"Isn't she beautiful?" said Jordy. "The **perfect** height and build for you."

"Come closer, Sophie, and get to know her," said Miss Jill.

Sophie walked forward and stretched out her hand. She slowly stroked the pony's golden coat. Jordy passed her the lead rope. Peaches' nostrils softened as she relaxed.

"We'll give Peaches some time to settle in," said Miss Jill. "Let's put her in the paddock with Gypsy Rose. I think those two will get along wonderfully."

Sophie led Peaches up to the paddock and through the gate. Gypsy Rose approached **cautiously**. She reached out her nose and whinnied quietly. She **sniffed** and **snickered**, bobbing her head and moving closer and closer to Peaches. Peaches snorted softly and shifted her weight from hoof to hoof.

Everyone held their breath.

Gypsy Rose had seen enough. She turned and wandered back to her favourite corner of the paddock. Peaches followed her and began to graze nearby.

"How are you feeling about coming back now, Sophie?" smiled Bella, as they watched their ponies becoming friends.

"I can't quite believe it," replied Sophie. "My cheeks hurt from **smiling**."

The following Saturday, Hannah, Sophie and Bella were in the tack room getting organised before riding class. Alexa and Lola appeared at the door. Lola **nudged** Alexa with her elbow and then looked away.

"Alright," whispered Alexa. She cleared her throat. "Um, well, I … I wanted to say sorry."

Bella, Hannah and Sophie looked at each other.

"I'm sorry I called you *borrowers.* Especially you, Sophie." Bella nodded and smiled. "It wasn't right. I can see that now. You and Biscuit were a great team and I'm sure you and Peaches will be great too."

"Gee thanks, Alexa," said Sophie. "I guess I should thank you for introducing Lola to Biscuit. It was a bit of a **shock** for me at first, but now I'm really glad Lola's riding him."

Alexa smiled but Lola nudged her again. The smile disappeared.

"Oh yes," said Alexa, pulling a brown paper bag from behind her back. "Please accept these with my apology. They're mints for the ponies."

"I give them to Biscuit when he's been jumping well," added Lola. "And Alexa gives them to Billy Blaze."

"Is that right?" teased Bella.

"Only **occasionally**," said Alexa, turning red.

"So that's your training secret!" said Hannah, smiling. "I'll try them on Jin Jin."

"Just don't give too many," said Alexa. "They are *treats*, remember."

"Yes, thank you, Alexa," said Bella.

"Oh, there's one more thing," said Alexa, pulling an **awkward face**. "I forgot to bring my riding helmet today. Very strange. I've never forgotten it before, so I need to … borrow one."

Bella was sure she saw a smile **flutter** across Lola's face.

"Borrow one?" repeated Hannah.

"I'll get one for you," Sophie said graciously. She handed Alexa a helmet.

"Thank you." Alexa and Lola turned and left. Lola waved as she went through the door.

"I hope that helmet will be alright on Alexa," said Sophie.

"It looked like the right size to me," said Hannah.

"I know," said Sophie, "but I think Alexa's head may have just shrunk a little with that apology."

"Well, I hope she likes the smaller size better," said Bella. "Come on, we don't want to be late for Peaches' first Saturday lesson."

"I wonder what Peaches will be like at jumping?" said Sophie. "I can't wait to find out!"

PONY PROFILE

Name: Biscuit

Riders: Sophie and Lola

Owner: Saddleback Stables

Age: 17

Breed: Shetland pony

Height: 10 hands

Temperament: playful, stubborn, caring

Coat: chestnut

Markings: one white sock on the near (pony's left) hind leg

Habits: nibbling on his bit, coming to a complete stop when he has had enough riding, tickling with his whiskers when patted

Likes: hugs, carrots, hanging out with Jin Jin

Dislikes: galloping, hot weather and competitions

Did you know? Shetland ponies are very hardy—that means they live a long time and can survive tough conditions. Shetlands often live 20 years or longer, through all kinds of weather. They must eat the right kinds of food. If they eat too many treats, they can get hoof problems.

GLOSSARY

bond
a close relationship

farrier
a person who makes and fits shoes to horses and ponies

halter
a rope or strap for leading a horse or pony

horse float
a van or trailer for moving horses and ponies by road

tiptop
excellent

whinny
the soft, high-pitched neigh of a horse or pony